THE
FOREST

CLAIRE A. NIVOLA

FRANCES FOSTER BOOKS

FARRAR STRAUS GIROUX

NEW YORK

Distributed in Canada by Douglas & McIntyre Ltd.

Color separations by Hong Kong Scanner Arts

Printed in the United States of America by Phoenix Color Corporation

Designed by Filomena Tuosto

First edition, 2002

1 3 5 7 9 10 8 6 4 2

Library of Congress Cataloging-in-Publication Data

Nivola, Claire A.

The forest / Claire A. Nivola.— 1st ed.

p. cm.

Summary: A mouse sets out to overcome a lifelong fear of the forest.

ISBN 0-374-32452-2

[1. Mice—Fiction. 2. Fear—Fiction. 3. Forests and forestry—Fiction.] I. Title.

PZ7.N6435 Fo 2002

[E]—dc21   00-46653

For Miriam, Hedda, Anne and Dan, and Rudi,
the beloved pillar trees of my forest

And for Tolstoy's Prince Andrei, who, fallen in battle,
looked up to see the "lofty, equitable, and kindly sky"
and understood so much

I HAD ALWAYS BEEN AFRAID OF THE FOREST, that dark and unknown place at the farthest edge of my little world. At night I often dreamed of it and woke chilled with fear. The fear was there in the day, too, hidden inside me no matter what I did or where I went.

One night the fear pressed so heavily on me that I could bear it no longer.

In the morning, standing in the doorway of my home, I saw the cozy chair by the fire, my warm bed, the objects I loved.

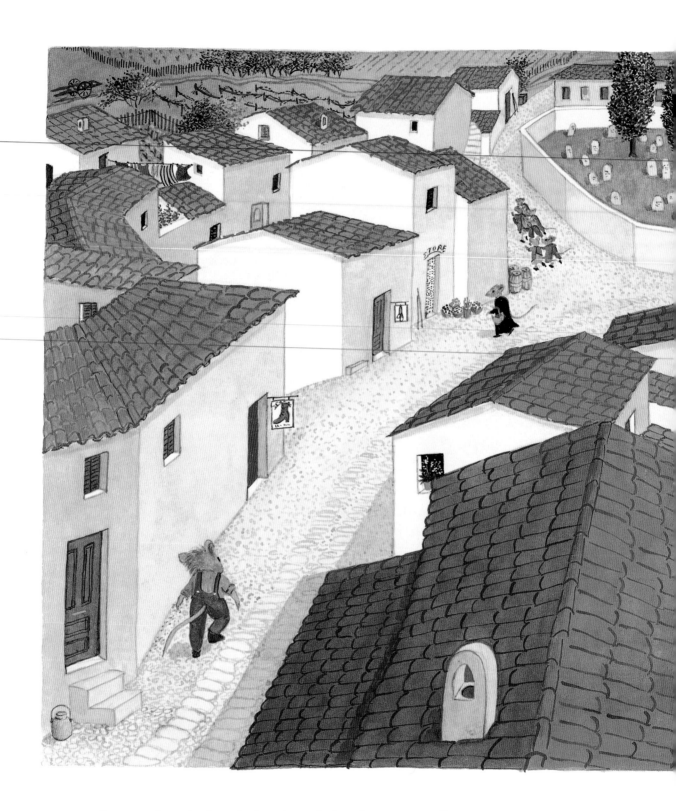

I turned and closed the door behind me. I walked through
the village that I knew like the back of my hand. I passed

the shops and houses laid out in their familiar order and
followed the long curve of the street.

On the high road, my heart began to race. I no longer felt like myself, but small and alone in the big world.

I walked on and on, past unknown farms and fields, until
the paved road ended.

Uneasy, I looked back at my village—a dot in the distance.

Looming before me, shaking its many heads slowly in the
wind, stood the forest.

Should I turn back? Should I run back, heart racing, to the safety of my house?

No, I had come too far.

But would I lose myself? Would I be devoured by some wild creature? Would I die of fear?

I stepped inside the forest, between two pillar trees that stood like a gateway.

My heart was pounding. A sharp birdcall from behind made me jump. Something cracked nearby, and a dark shadow moved swiftly toward me, coming closer and closer. Leaping for cover, I tripped and fell headlong to the ground. Lie still, I thought; if you cry or move, you will be found. Could my thundering heart be heard outside my head?

When I opened my eyes, my nose was deep in moss, a forest of tiny trees, as soft as feathers. The sunlight was raining down through the leaves and warming my back. A sweet breeze stirred my fur.

I was alive!

How long had I been here?

A butterfly opened and shut its wings nearby, like a guardian angel.

I listened. All around me a million leaves whispered and rustled gently. I rolled over and, for the first time, looked up.

High above, I saw the sky. The sky was bigger than the forest, bigger even than my fear had been, bigger than everything.

I lay there—a speck in this enormous beauty—until the light began to fade.

Then, with the sweet murmuring world of the forest filling me, I walked the long way home.